Dear Mr. Thoreau

Claire Russell

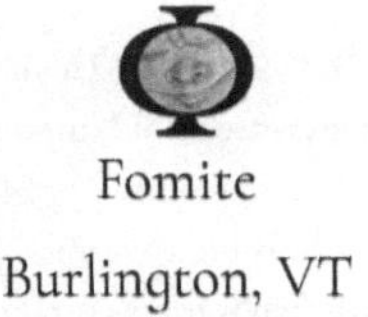

Fomite

Burlington, VT

ISBN: 978-1-953236-14-2

Library of Congress Control Number: 2020945857

Fomite

Burlington, VT

http://www.fomitepress.com

This is a work of epistolary fiction involving Henry David Thoreau, his real-life friends and family and the fictional Mary Bright and hers.

To Henry,

beyond the beyond, ever and anon.

And to

Ellery Channing,

Henry's closest friend and favorite walking companion.

To my son Alex who cleared the path

and to my son Adrian who lit the way.

Dear Mr. Thoreau,

My name is Mary. My last name is Bright so I am
Mary Bright. I am eleven years old. Fanny says you walk
a lot every day. Sometimes she sees you when she goes
to the market. You are always in a hurry she says to get
somewhere on your long walks. Mama tells her not to
gossip and to mind who she's talking to, a child who could
go telling tales, especially about a kind man like Mr.
Thoreau. I mean no unkindness Mr. Thoreau. I am curious
about you that is all. Where do you go when you walk? Is
it far away? Do you get tired?

I go to the woods alone sometimes because I love the
trees and birds, just everything and it is so peaceful there.
There are dark places even on a sunny day and once when
I was there with James, he's my big brother, I said I heard
music. He said no I was imagining it. What a silly goose
you are he said.

Mama says to stop writing now. Don't trouble Mr.
Thoreau any longer with foolish tales she says. You will
take up too much of his time. Mr. Thoreau has important
surveying work to do for the town she says. I asked Mama
how to spell surveying and what it meant.

Mr. Thoreau do you think you will have time to
write me? I would like that very much. You can leave a

letter to Miss Mary Bright at the post office. Mama or Papa can collect it for me or maybe even James if he is not being hateful.

Your friend,
Mary Bright

P.S. I want you to know that I don't think you are a crank or lazy as some people say but not Mama or Papa. Or Fanny.

Dear Miss Mary Bright,

What an unexpected pleasure it was to receive such a delightful letter! Should I address you as Miss Bright or would you prefer that I call you Mary? I prefer Mary, and would like you to call me Henry with your mama and papa's permission. They might think it is not right to address someone older than you by their Christian name unless properly introduced to you first. Just ask them how they feel about it and we will abide by their decision. Well, enough of this silly business about names and what to call each other.

I read your letter with great interest, especially the part about hearing music while walking in the woods with your brother James. He called you a silly goose, did he? Just between you and me I hear music in the woods too. Maybe he should call me a silly goose as well.

I go on very long walks every day after spending my mornings reading and writing unless I have work that needs my attention. I go where my feet lead me and the rest of me just seems to fall into step, happy to let them take the lead. Do I get tired? I've never asked myself that question so I have no answer for you. I am too busy to give it much thought, looking at everything that is around me and enjoying the experience.

I will close this letter now and get to my surveying work which has been keeping me busy the last few days. Thank you for your letter Miss Mary Bright. I hope to hear from you again soon.

Your friend,
Henry Thoreau

P.S. Just between us being called a crank and lazy does not bother me at all. I would be in a sorry state if I let the opinions of others disturb me even a little bit.

Dear Henry,

I asked Mama and she says that I may call you Henry instead of Mr. Thoreau so I will. She said you helped Papa clean the barn once and painted a fence for him too and that Papa says you are a good worker, so maybe that is why I can call you Henry instead of Mr. Thoreau.

Mama says I can invite you for tea and cakes at 12:30 tomorrow afternoon so that I can meet you. Please say you will come. James wants to show you his new fish pole, even though I can see nothing special about it.

I'm going to help Fanny make the cakes. It is my first try at baking, so I am a bit nervous about it. Anyway you can wash them down with tea if you must and I won't mind.

Your friend,
Mary Bright

P.S. It is my opinion that you need a friend.

Dear Mary,

I am very much looking forward to meeting you and to sample your fine tea cakes which I am sure I will not have to wash down with tea, but thank you for the tip. I will be at your house at 12:30 tomorrow. Since you helped prepare the cakes, perhaps you would be so kind as to share the recipe so that I can pass it on to *my* mama?

Henry

P.S. Maybe we can take a walk someday soon and find the music that you heard in the woods. Let's ask your mama when I see you tomorrow. Mary, I feel that friends are ever in demand and always in short supply and so I will always welcome and be grateful for a new one.

Dear Betsy,

Mr. Thoreau came to our house today for tea and cakes. I will call him Henry from now on because Mama says I may but you cannot since you do not know him. Anyway, I cannot decide for sure what to think, besides the fact that he is very polite and has very good manners. I should not judge him too harshly, but he is a bit short and rough looking if you know what I mean. He looks like a vagabond, but anyway he is a very nice one. I think he is out of doors much of the day so that is probably why he looks the way he does. His face is nice, but all weather-worn and colored from the sun. He did wear a frock coat which to my mind looked a bit silly because it didn't seem to suit him and he *did* seem a bit uncomfortable — but Mama would scold me for saying so. She will hear no criticism of him at all, even if it is meant in a kindly way. Can criticism ever be kind? I don't know. Anyway, that is what I thought.

We are going for a walk soon, Henry and I, so I must close this letter. I'll be thinking of you as you sit in the parlor with your embroidery.

Mary

Dear Mary,

I wouldn't dream of calling Mr. Thoreau "Henry". Whyever would you think it? I must say I am shocked that your mama gave her permission for you to do so but it is not for me to say.

I have seen your Mr.Thoreau at the post office once or twice and I think him rather handsome. Anyway I must say you seemed a bit too critical of him and yes I think it is a bit unkind. A vagabond indeed!

Betsy

P.S. My embroidery is coming along nicely. I don't go wandering in the woods, except for those few times with you. It is either too cold and damp or too warm to suit me. I stay at home where I belong. You might consider that Miss Mary. Your needlework is a shambles.

Dear Betsy,

My needlework *is* a shambles and I do not care if it is. I have other interests but let's not quarrel over such a trifle, dear. You are my best friend and I would not have us argue for any reason especially over something silly like embroidery.

So you think Henry is handsome. I cannot credit it but will look more closely at him when next he and I are together. You must see something in him that I do not.

Mary

Dear Henry,

I've already asked Mama about going for a walk after tea and cakes and she says we can go if I finish my chores. I will get them done in a flash. James says that sometimes. He says a lot of things like that, 'in a flash'.

I'm saving some of my cake to give to someone tomorrow. You'll see who when we go for our walk.

Your new friend, Mary, and I understand.

Dear Mary,

I thank you for sharing your discovery with me. It was a kind and generous thing to do.

This is just a letter to remind you of what we talked about, to keep listening, believing, and you will without a doubt hear many more remarkable things as you continue your woodland walks. But do seek out other places as well. I don't think we spoke much about that.

There are fields and meadows, swamps and streams that are just waiting for you, all with unique sounds and sights to delight you. Everything in nature, and there is so much of her to explore, will yield herself to your eyes, your ears and heart. You will hear different voices, different music wherever you go, for rivers, lakes, streams, swamps, fields and woods have their own unique spells to weave for those who are aware. Be open to all of it and you will be all the better for it.

Henry

Dear Henry,

I *do* want to do more exploring. Sometimes I walk with my friend Betsy in the woods even though she doesn't care for it much because she is always fussing about her shoes getting dirty. I don't care about my shoes getting dirty at all, even if Mama scolds me for it.

I took Betsy to our secret place a few days past because I wanted to share it with her as I did with you. I waited for her to say something about the music, but she said nothing at all. When we went back to her house I didn't know what to talk about so I came home. I was sure she would hear what you and I hear, but she didn't. She is my best friend, so she must have heard it. If she did not maybe it will be hard to be friends with her, for we will have nothing important to talk about. I am very sad about it.

Mary

Dear Mary,

I understand how disappointed you are. I have felt, many times, that I wish my best friend could see what I see, could hear what I hear. But then I say to myself, "Well, Henry, and what if he could? Would he not be a copy of you, another Henry? Is that what you would want or expect in a friend? Is it not better that he would have a new and interesting point of view to share, something that perhaps you cannot see or hear, that he can? Perhaps a different shade of a flower that you have seen many times before, or an unusual shape of a red oak leaf or the song of a wood thrush that has, perchance, an extra note in his beautiful melodic song that you have failed to hear but your friend has heard and can describe the sound of it to you? What a gift that would be!

Let Betsy show you what *she* has noticed when you are together and I assure you it will be a surprise. You will see that world through *her* eyes, not yours. The voices and music that you and I hear will always be there for us, never fear. Let's be thankful for that and not concern ourselves with who hears and sees what and who does not.

Henry

P.S. Forgive me if I sound a bit preachy in this letter, Mary. That is the way I express myself at times, and I do not mean to offend you.

Dear Henry,

I am going to market with Fanny today. Mama says it is time for me to learn some things that all girls of my age should know. I don't see why, because Fanny is the one who cooks and cleans for us, but I will be a dutiful daughter and not complain.

I am less cross about Betsy today, but I was cross with myself for feeling that I am better than she is just because I can hear some sounds in the woods that she cannot. She and I have many things to do that we enjoy very much, so you will be glad to hear that I will dwell on those things that we have in common.

Adieu for now,
Mary

P.S. You have my permission to be preachy, but I do hope that you will be a little less so than Mama and Papa.

Dear Mary,

You were thoughtful in your dilemma with Betsy and arrived at a very mature decision, thinking with both your head and your heart about how much this friendship means to both of you. I am very proud of you.

What say you to this, with your mama's permission? When you are home from the market will you be ready for a little adventure? I have some work to attend to myself, some fence repair for a neighbor, but I will be free this afternoon.

Send a message to the house if you cannot come and I will get it when I return home for a bit of dinner. If you *are* free, I will leave the adventure up to you, either by foot or by sail in my boat, perhaps a bit of both and I will come to fetch you around 1:00.

Henry

Dear Henry,

Mama says yes, I may go. My chores are finished for the day and I can come with you this afternoon. Can we go sailing please? I've never been in a boat before. Did you make it yourself? Is it very big? I will be waiting for you by the gate at 1:00.

Mary

Dear Mary,

My brother John and I built the boat. We named it the *Musketaquid,* the Indian name for what we now call our Concord river.

You will have to decide for yourself if it is big, but you will see it is just the right size for you and me and one or two more. My mother and sister Sophia love the river, so we sail or I row and we make a pleasant afternoon of it as often as we can.

I think you will like the colors that John and I chose for the *Musketaquid.* We painted it blue and green to honor our fish and bird friends who swim in the water and fly in the sky or fly in the water and swim in the sky. I like to imagine it both ways.

Until 1:00 then,
Henry

Dear Betsy,

I went sailing with Henry today. It was heavenly. We were on the Concord river but Henry said it used to be called the Musketaquid named so by the Indians. This is the first time I have ever been sailing and I hope we go often for I do love it. Henry and his brother built the boat themselves and painted it blue and green like the water and the sky. His brother died a few years ago and it still seems to pain Henry to speak of him so I didn't ask much about him.

Shall I ask Henry if you can come with us the next time we go? It would be such fun to have you along with us. There is plenty of room and Henry would be most happy to have you join us I am sure.

Mary

P.S. I still don't see him handsome and I did look hard, quite staring at him when he was not aware of it.

Dear Mary,

I will be occupied next week, possibly as long as a fortnight with surveying that will take me outside the boundaries of the village. The only rambling I do will be with my surveyor's compass and chain and other tools of the trade.

I'll send you a note when I return so that we can do some *real* rambling, the kind that satisfies and puts a spring in one's step.

Henry

P.S. I am glad you like the *Musketaquid*. She is a good companion and a faithful friend. You are a very good ship's mate for one who had never been on a boat before and I will be proud to be your captain on all expeditions we undertake in the future.

Dear Mary,

That sail with Mr. Thoreau sounds quite thrilling. I do like your descriptions of the boat and the significance of the colors. How imaginative of Mr. Thoreau and his brother to think of such things as birds and fish when choosing them. I feel dreadfully sorry for him, for losing his brother the way he did. My mama and papa spoke of it and it went the rounds in the village, but I will not speak of it to you if you do not know the details. It is too horrible to relate.

As for joining you for a sail, I think not. I get quite giddy even looking at moving water on a river or a pond so you must excuse me. You are much more adventurous than I — which you remind me of quite often.

I look forward to seeing you, dear, on Tuesday next. I believe that is when we had planned a little party for the mamas to show off our skills in the kitchen, such as they are. Do bring your tea cakes for they are my especial favorites. I will try for something more substantial but have no idea as yet what it will be.

Au revoir,
Betsy

Dear Henry,

I hope your surveying wasn't too hard. Mama says what happens with your work is none of my concern and that I risk being impertinent. She spelled that word for me and made sure that I put it in this letter. I wish she would not look over my shoulder but she said to say this since I am writing to you. You are invited to dinner at 1:00 any day at your convenience. I say please come as soon as you can. We can have some more important talks, maybe on a walk and you can show me some more of your favorite places.

Mary

Dear Mary,

I accept the invitation to dine with you and your family with many thanks. I should be finishing with surveying tomorrow so I will be able to join you on Wednesday the 19th. And just between us you were not impertinent at all. Surveying is never hard. It takes a lot of time and is slow going sometimes if I have to wade through a swamp or some very dense woods, but I am out of doors and that makes all the difference to me. Work like that is not a hardship as it would be if I were confined behind a desk or a counter in a shop.

I spotted James at Flints Pond yesterday, when I was taking a much needed walk near there, a little break from work.

He had quite a mess of fish he had caught and was about to leave for home when I met up with him. We had some good conversations about fishing and other things that were of interest to him. He said his favorite place to be is with your Uncle John helping out on his farm, so we talked a lot about that. He loves it all, even mucking out the barns which I imagine all but the most committed to that kind of life would find most disagreeable.

One day maybe he'll have a piece of land of his own to grow wheat or corn or oats, cows and chickens perchance, maybe an orchard to round things off, some fine apple or peach trees. Being stuck behind a desk as shopkeeper or banker seems as hard a path for James as it would be for me.

I will see you soon,
Henry

Dear Henry,

You'll never guess what I found on my bed this morning, all laid out as pretty as can be! My very first party dress! It is the palest blue color you have ever seen like the most beautiful summer sky with a dark blue sash and there are new shoes and gloves to match.

I forgot to say. I have been invited to a party, by a friend of Betsy who wants to meet me. I confess I am reluctant to go, but Betsy will be coming so I won't be too nervous with her there.

It is afternoon now. I had to stop writing for awhile because Mama gave me some terrible news. James was going to take me to the party because Papa said he had to, but he is visiting cousin George and he will not be able to return home in time. He is helping our Uncle with the haying and cannot leave the work half done. There is no one on the farm but James and George to do it because Uncle John is feeling poorly and Papa will not let me attend the party without James.

I am feeling quite poorly myself at this bad news. My beautiful dress will go to waste, for I won't be able to wear it any time soon. There are no more parties and I am broken-hearted.

Mary

Dear Miss Mary,

I cannot let you remain broken-hearted. Your papa and I have come up with a plan that will remedy the situation.

Are you ready for good news? After I received your last letter I paid a call on your father and he has agreed to let me accompany you to the party. He has not spoken of it to you because he wanted it to be a surprise which I hope it is, a very happy one.

We will be traveling in a carriage that belongs to a kind friend who will let us have the use of it for the evening. It is quite a distance to walk and you would ruin your pretty new dancing slippers before you got proper use out of them and the young men at the party would have a sad time of it if they could not take a turn around the floor with you. So we will arrive at the party in style with my clean shoes and your clean slippers to boot.

Henry

P.S. There is one condition that I respectfully request as your escort. I reserve the right to have one dance with you, any one of which you may choose.

Dear Henry,

You have come to my rescue like a prince from a fairy tale, coach and all! I thank you with all my heart and Papa too for giving you permission to escort me to the party. I believe I am happier than I have ever been in my life and you are the dearest and best of friends!

Mama said you were to bring me home at a respectable hour, whatever that means. Perhaps you should ask her, though I'm sure she will tell you before you have a chance to get the words out.

I would like to arrive at the party at 7:00, but come a bit early if you can. Anyway, it is probably proper for a chaperone, which Mama says you are, to give last minute instructions which hopefully will not last more than a *short* minute. I will listen to you for that length of time but no longer.

Joyfully,
Mary

My dear Miss Mary,

A short minute, you say. Less than that, I assure you. I will be a proper, for I take this responsibility very seriously, but very liberal chaperone, you can count on it. As I was coming up short on quite a few of the daily good deeds I had promised myself to fulfill, accompanying you to the party took care of a number of them quite handily.

Henry

Dear Henry,

You made a most wonderful prince and chaperone. I don't think Mama and Papa quite understood how important it was to me to attend this party. I don't have many friends at home, but now I know Jane Althorp, Betsy's friend, the one who wanted to meet me, and many other most agreeable girls, perhaps a boy or two as well. It was truly the most fun I have ever had, dancing and games and just everything, but most importantly, meeting Jane, my new friend, and her family.

I did not see much of you there. I hope the evening was not too tiresome for you and that you found some way to keep boredom at bay.

A grateful Mary

P.S. May we walk again soon or will you be working?

Dear Betsy,

I think the party was wonderful, just *glorious*! I had the best time in the world! There was that game that Jane Althorp proposed. I can't remember the name. I have never played it before but hope we do so again at the next party. Jane's brother Bradford was an especially good player. I can't imagine why he chose me for a partner, but it turned out well for our side because we won.

You *do* know that Henry brought me to the party because James is away working at my uncle's farm. It is only because of Henry's kindness that I was able to attend because Papa would not let me go without someone to accompany me. He is my very own prince and perhaps will take me to future parties as well.

Adieu for now,
Mary

Dear Mary,

I confess I was surprised to find myself enjoying the evening so much, so you needn't concern yourself on that account. It was *your* night Mary, not mine but as I was preparing to take a stroll out of doors I met a most congenial fellow who turned out to be none other than your new friend's father, a Mr. David Althorp. I have heard of him, of course. He is well known for his just and liberal views on education, even, I believe, an acquaintance of both Mr. Emerson and Mr. Alcott, a most interesting man whose ideas I hold very dear. We had a pleasant time of it talking about many things of interest to both of us, and he took me on a walk around the grounds where we spent a good deal of time among the flower gardens, especially the roses which are singular favorites of his. I don't believe I have ever seen such glorious colors, as if the roses themselves were proud to put on a display for our particular pleasure.

What a blessing to have such loveliness when thoughts may turn to things unpleasant or on a blustery winter day when we don't have such summery beauty to remind us of the warm days ahead.

I propose that we take a walk as soon as possible. It has been a long time since we have done so and I have no work projects at present.

I am available most afternoons, so Miss Mary, propose a time and I will be at your service unless something unforeseen occurs between now and then.

Henry

P.S. Ah, I see by your postscript that I must have overlooked in a too hasty reading of your letter that you also want to go for a walk. With your mama's permission, shall we try for a longer one, what I would call a _short saunter_ that might include a sail as well? I would not want her to worry about you returning home later than usual.

Dear Henry,

I will be ready at 1:00 sharp tomorrow, if it is not too short notice for you. You may call for me then for our short saunter. Mama said yes and will have a picnic basket for us with vegetables from the garden, boiled eggs, bread and a fresh baked apple pie if that suits you and the sun is kind enough to shine on us.

Let us hope for a good day tomorrow with no bad weather or anything that could spoil our walk *and* sail.

Mary

P.S. I am so glad that you met Mr. Althorp. Jane introduced me to him and I like him very much. I also met Jane's brother Bradford, and he chose me to be his partner in a very fun game and we won! I would trade James for him at once if I could for he is very kind and attentive to his sister.

Dear Mary,

I will call upon you tomorrow at 1:00. I might be a minute or so late, as you might have noticed, but I have no way of reckoning the precise time to anyone's satisfaction since I have no time piece with which to chart the passage of the hours and something unforeseen *has* come up, a small task for Mrs. Emerson that requires attention. Perhaps we should meet at 1:30 instead. Then I will be sure to be free. A picnic lunch seems to be exactly what is called for, and I would be obliged if you would pass on my thanks and gratitude to your kind mama.

If it does rain, we will have our picnic indoors at my house where you will be greeted with as much affection as you can stand by my mother who thinks of you as her own little chick, just hatched from the egg. I have spoken about you often, you see, and she has made you one of the family, which in my opinion is a very good thing. You will see what I mean when you meet her and my sister Sophia.

Henry

Dear Betsy,

Henry wants me to meet his mother and sister
Sophia. Do you not think that is a very great courtesy? I
confess it is quite unexpected. We are picnicking if there
is no rain, but I am sure Henry will present me to them
when we return from our walk. He says he speaks often
of me, that I am almost one of the family. I do feel quite
honored to be considered so. I do begin to see a little of
what you see in him, though more from a distance than
close up.

Mary

Dear Henry,

I think our walk and sail and picnic yesterday was magical. How wonderful that the weather cooperated for us. Have you ever heard so many birds singing so gloriously? Why, the notes just poured from their throats all in a-jumble, making the most beautiful music I have ever heard. I am quite sure I heard *our* music as well. What a wonderful accompaniment to the little feathered creatures who were making so merry in the treetops.

Henry, where does the music come from? What is it? We have talked often about hearing it but not how it comes to be in the first place. It is such a mystery and I would like to know what you think.

Mary

Dear Mary,

Let me propose this: What we hear, that perfect
accompaniment as you say, for the birds' singing that
thrilled us is perchance *celestial* music created by the wind,
by water, the songs of the beings who live in hidden dells
away from paths worn smooth by human feet, maybe
by other things of which we have no knowledge. But let
us assign no name or look too deeply, for sometimes the
mystery of a thing is what enchants us and we should
look no further than what we can see or hear with our
own eyes and ears. Words, the attempt to label something
we experience as sacred, puts a cage around the very thing
that is meant to be free, limits it and creates boundaries
in our minds to curb our enjoyment of it — and I would
not have it so.

As to where the music seems to *come* from there is
no way to know for sure and is it necessary that we do? Is
it a particular place? Does it live in the air? We can only
guess. Let's put our faith in *believing* instead of knowing
and that will be a better thing.

Henry

Dear Betsy,

I am all fluttery inside and I have to speak of it to you, my dearest friend. Henry and I went to our special place in the woods and heard the most wonderful things, the glorious singing of birds and I do believe, though I know you do not, music from somewhere else that has no place or name. Henry would not have it so, for he says that naming it is like putting a cage around something that should be free. I begin to understand him more and more, the longer I am with him.

Adieu,
Mary

Dear Henry,

Do you remember when I told you James called me a " silly goose?" It seems so long ago now when I think of it. He didn't hear the music voices and I almost doubted my own senses. He is my older brother, after all. I believed him and was almost convinced to call *myself* a "silly goose".

I have learned much from you since then, recalling my disappointment about Betsy, and how our friends and family can show us different things that they experience that *we* do not see or hear.

Yesterday James and I went fishing. I have never wanted to go with him. Fishing quite puts me off. But we so seldom do things together I consented. I was shocked that he asked me to go with him, certainly curious. I confess I was surprised when my brother waxed quite poetic about it. He spoke of the shadings of color in the water, the trees bending over the river as if to embrace it, even the beauty of the fish themselves what he called the "comeliness" of their shape. I had to remind myself that I was with James and not you at those moments.

This is a James I have never seen before. Maybe I am just growing up yet I I would stay a young girl as long as possible without the concerns that older people have which seem so unimportant to me. You, dear Mr. Thoreau will never be old. You are young still and wonderfully silly and terribly wise even when you get preachy with me.

I am going to Boston tomorrow with Mama to visit my Aunt Lydia and Uncle Ezra. I have only been once before so I am looking forward to it very much.

I will send you a note when I return, for I expect that I will have much to tell you. I will miss you and our walks.

Mary

Dear Mary,

I am going on a journey myself, but to a mountain rather than a city. A friend is visiting me, a Mr. Blake coming all the way from Worcester. We will spend a night or two on Mt. Wachusett with a tent, bed roll, and fire for company, and return home later in the week. I hope to do some botanizing as well, but the weather gods will have to cooperate for me to do a proper job of it. They are a fickle bunch but perhaps I can charm them with my flute. It has worked before and I am holding out hope it will work again if necessary. But friend Blake and I will enjoy ourselves whatever comes our way, with much needed time away from our family responsibilities and a bit of the wild thrown in for good measure.

Lest I forget to mention it, I read with interest and a glad heart, the recounting of your time spent with James. Perhaps more opportunities will present themselves in the future. Sophia and I spend some pleasant hours together when we can, but she has teaching responsibilities and I am occupied with my writing, walking, sailing, &c and my dear sister declares them to be right and good uses of my time. She is as much a dear friend as a sister. Perhaps that is what is happening between you and James as well now that you are getting older and you will find more interests to share with each other.

Upon occasion the odd job seeks me out here and there and, despite my best attempts to become invisible, I find I must give in after all. My family does benefit from the bit of money that I bring to the table, so I complain little and tackle my responsibilities as a good son and brother must. Do not believe too much in my protestations about work, for I take to it easily as long as I am not confined indoors overmuch. Honest hard work is good for the soul as well as the body, and both of mine need a challenging work-out on a regular basis.

We can tell each other about our adventures when next we meet, but for now I'm going to the woods at Walden pond to study a patchwork quilt of lichens on some pines that caught my eye, and without a doubt I will see other wonders as well.

Henry

Dear Betsy,

The trip to Boston was enjoyable. Mama and I saw some interesting sites, but I won't bore you with details. You'll never guess who we met quite by chance at the station? It was Bradford Althorp of all people! He had been visiting friends in Boston and was returning home on the same train. Mama insisted that we sit together but she was across from us of course. He was extremely complimentary about my new bonnet which pleased me exceedingly. I think better of him each time I see him, for he is a gentleman to be sure, though he doesn't quite rise to the level of Henry in that regard.

Well, I must close this and pen a letter to Henry, as I promised him that I would write when I returned home. You and I must get together as soon as possible. I did miss our talks when I was away.

Mary

Dear Henry,

Boston was wonderful, so much to see. I will let you know more if you wish it. I did love the Athenaeum and saw your Harvard school. I would love to have had a tour of the classrooms and have spent more time walking on the grounds, but I imagined you there and that had to satisfy me.

There was an unexpected surprise waiting for us as we were about to board the train home. Bradford Althorp was there! He had been visiting family friends in Boston so Mama and I sat with him and we had a very enjoyable ride. The Althorp family is coming on Friday for a light supper which I am going to help prepare. I am a bit nervous about it, but I can rely on dear Fanny to help me over any rough spots.

Mary

P.S. I would love a saunter with you. Let's meet here at say 2:00 tomorrow? If not convenient just send a message.

Dear Mary,

I confess you have seen more of Boston with just two visits than I have, so I was very interested to hear what you thought. When I go there most of my time is spent at the public library though I have taken a turn around the city a time or two. I give little if any thought to my years spent at Harvard, but that is just my prejudice, having been an indifferent student while there, surely due to boredom and lack of inspiration.

Concord must seem like a very sleepy place to you compared to such a big city with so many things to experience, so many places to go. I do believe, however, that you and I have the same thoughts about this, that Boston is exciting, but Concord is the most congenial place to live.

Alas, my plans for botanizing came to naught at Mt. Wachusett. It did indeed rain, something like what Noah must have experienced as he set about building his Ark. All that was missing were the pairs of every living creature mandated by God, else surely friend Blake and I would have been present day participants reliving some very ancient history.

Henry

P.S. It must have been a happy meeting with Bradford Althorp on the way back home from Boston, though you didn't say much about it when I saw you. Do not fret about your supper with the Althorps. I think that Bradford will be less interested in the meal and more in the young lady that helped prepare it.

Dear Wise Man,

Yes, supper with the Althorp family was very successful. The best part of it was when we all played a lively game of charades, Bradford, Jane, James and I pitting ourselves against our worthy but not very skillful parents.

The liveliness was all on our side as one by one our elders went down in defeat. To show what good sports they were the mamas made hot chocolate to serve with the dessert cakes as the papas broke into song to cheer them on. It was such fun, Henry, but I could not help wishing that you had been there. Your presence would have made the evening complete.

Mary

Dear Channing,

I am at a loss as to how to proceed with this letter.
I am out of my depth here. I would prefer to see you and
speak of this but I don't know when next we meet, you
being with Ricketson for an extended period of time and
my family obligations that keep me here. I will get *to* it
then. Please do not let your mind drift to thoughts of an
unsavory nature if you can help it which of course you
can if you so choose.

Do you recall my speaking of Mary Bright, the
young girl that I have been corresponding with for a
year or so, maybe more? I don't measure time with much
accuracy unless I am called upon to do so with a project
that calls for attention to such details so it is a guess
on my part, but she is now fourteen years of age so you
can figure it out for yourself. She is a girl becoming a
woman, Channing, and I sense her interest in me has
taken a turn from that of being a friend platonic to
something that is alarming in the extreme. Her letters to
me are completely respectable should they perchance be
seen by straying eyes if left unattended on her writing
desk, but her demeanor when we are together for our
walks or picnics or whatever it is we decide to do on
a particular day has taken on a more familiar aspect

toward me. She takes my arm as we walk, she gazes at me with a frankness and warmth that I have not seen from her before. I see it all unfolding, what looks dangerous to me, an uncompromising attitude in her that is disarming in one so young.

This is a *girl*, Channing, exceptional though she is, she is still a *girl*. I could be her father, and I fear that what is happening will continue and get more complicated in the days to come, going somewhere where I would not have it go. There is a young man of whom she speaks, a Bradford Althorp, and she holds him in very high esteem. He is a new acquaintance, the young son of Mr. David Althorp, a highly respected member of the community as are all the members of his large family. So perhaps I make too much of an issue that does not exist. My hopes are that she will find him agreeable and either pursue him or let him pursue her. Either way would satisfy me completely. That being said, with all of these changes I confess that I will not suspend my walks with her unless she wishes to do so, nor any time spent with her, for everything I do with her is precious to me. I confess I do not even begin to understand myself these days.

I await your reply to this letter, one which I never thought I would be obliged to write.

Yours,

Thoreau

Forgive please the apparent contradictions in my
thoughts as I expressed them to you but I can assure you I
am more confused than you are.

My Dear Thoreau,

I am still trying to absorb what you are saying,
trying to fit myself into your mind which is a hard
thing to do, even for me, one who knows you so well.
To navigate my way into your heart is impossible. You
live there alone and have made it a condition of our
friendship, have you not, that I am not allowed access
to you there even when you most need my help, not that
I recall you ever asking for it. How can I help you then,
Thoreau, for all of your deepest most profound agonies
live there in that sad, yearning and restless place along
with all that is most tranquil and at peace inside you.
Quite a potent mix, my friend.

My first thoughts are not worthy of the profound
seriousness that I sense from the tone of your letter, but I
will say them and you can rail at me from a distance now
and then when next I see you in person I give you leave to
strike me if you must. I will be the unpardonable Ellery
now, the one that most annoys, shocks and frustrates you,
the irreverent Ellery because I want you to meet me even
here in this letter, to hear me through that haze of anger
and despair that sometimes has you in its grip

You know what I would do with this young lady or
at least what I would attempt. I have no scruples in this

regard nor in much else, but you know that already. Of
course you will not taint yourself or this girl by any carnal
activity outside the limits of what is considered proper
and conventional, not even suggest it to her, though she
might consent with but a little persuasion on your part.
You say you will not give up your time with her. Then pay
the emotional consequences, my friend. If she falls in love
with you, I pity her for you are unavailable to her and to
any woman because of your abiding and in my opinion,
misguided love for Ellen Sewall.

But perhaps you have misread it all, as you say,
and this potential drama that is unfolding is of no
consequence. You mentioned a young man that Miss
Bright is interested in. I think that is the way out for you,
Thoreau, for both of you. She will soon see, if she has
not done so already, that you are not good for her and
someone is there who can carry her away to a far better
life in the future than she would have had with you.

I am sad for you. You are wounded so deeply, as
deeply as I am, thus I fear that you cannot be mended.

Channing

Dear Henry,

We have just heard that my cousin Anne passed away three days ago. She is but twenty-two. I will not believe it Henry. We will be leaving for Salem immediately. I will let you know when I return.

Mary

Dearest girl,

Please know that I am here, that I will come to you if you but whisper my name. I have sent a note to your mother and father as well and will come to offer any help I can to ease their way during this hard time.

I believe the garden might need tending and I can surely lend a hand there and with anything else that must be dealt with. I expect to hear from your father this afternoon when he stops by the house on the way back from town. We will discuss anything else that needs to be done.

I will wait to hear from you on your return, Mary. You and your family are ever in my thoughts.

Henry

Dear Blake,

Forgive the short notice, but I must cancel my lecture. There has been a death in the family of friends who are dear to me and I must be of service to them in any way I can while they are away and if they need me when they return. Again, my apologies for the abrupt change of plans. I will let you know when I am available.

HDT

Dear Henry,

I feel as if a piece of my heart is gone and I will never be whole again. I do not believe I will ever recover from this loss, for Anne was a sister to me. She lived with us for a time when my Aunt Charlotte was sick, and we spent most of our earliest years together even after my aunt regained her health. We could not bear to be parted and Mama and Papa loved her as one of their own, so Aunt consented to let her stay for a full two years before sending for her to return home.

I know how much you care for me and my family, but I am asking you not to send me a letter upon my return full of soothing words and common expressions of sympathy. I could not bear it and if you do not heed my words I will not be able to see you for a very long time.

Mary

Dear Henry,

I know Mama and Papa have expressed their thanks and gratitude to you for all that you did for us while we were in Salem. You know how I feel and my silent words must suffice. James is lucky to be at school away from all the sadness here. Anne was also like a sister to him, but I know that she meant more to him than that. It pains him even to speak her name, for I know that there was an understanding between them kept secret from both of our families until they were both older and could marry.

Do you remember when James asked me to come fishing with him some months ago? That is when he confided in me and told me of their future plans. I promised on my word of honor that I would keep silent about it and so I have. I was so surprised and grateful that he chose to confide in me. We have been so close ever since. I think Mama may have guessed something, for she has been especially tender to James these last weeks, though nothing has been said on either side. But mamas have a way of knowing things that defy explanation and ours is no different in that regard, except being even more perceptive than usual, too much so in my opinion.

Mama insists on having a celebration for my 15th birthday. She says it will be the perfect antidote to the gloom that has settled over our household. I feel unfit for any kind of celebrating, I do not think it is right, but she will not hear my protestations. I don't know if I can bear it without you, so please come.

Do you remember my first party, the one where I wore my pretty blue dress and you were the prince doubling as chaperone? It seems so long ago. To persuade you to come I am inviting my friends who would love to hear about your trip to Maine, Mama and Papa as well, so please say yes. I know little about it myself for you haven't said much about it to me. Perhaps you thought I wouldn't be interested, but I assure you I am. Jane and Bradford Althorp will be there and Betsy, of course.

I am reminded that I have to tell you the day and time. The day is Saturday the 12th, anytime after 5:00 P.M. We will dine at 6:00, just our family and you before the party. Perhaps we will have a quiet moment alone before my friends arrive.

Mary

P.S. I assume you will walk here, no fancy carriage like my first party, so no puddle splashing if you please. It has been quite rainy the last few days and I know how pools of water in the road draw you like a magnet.

Will you wear the frock coat that you wore when you were my prince chaperone? It will remind me of better times and at the risk of embarrassing you I must say that I think you looked very stylish, even, one might even say elegant. As you read these last words I believe I can feel you shudder all the way from your house to mine.

Dearest Girl,

With all of my heart I say this to you: Yes, it is not only right to celebrate your birthday after losing Anne, it is essential for you to do it, despite your grief. You are here with us, a part of us, and we need you. We need you to participate with us in the big moments, like your birthday party and even, maybe most importantly, in the small moments, everyday things like doing your chores, helping your mother as she works to bring order to the sometimes chaotic business of running a household. But fun things, too, like the times we spend together walking and talking and laughing and having tea at your house or mine, experiencing the magic of the wonderful music we hear on our walks in the woods.

Forgive me for giving such a long answer to a short comment that you made in your letter. I risk sounding *preachy* and that is far from my intention, so here is the short one: Have your party and enjoy every wonderful moment. Live your life as if Anne were still here, for she would want you to do that. Is that not the simplest and best reason of all? Answer that question from your heart and you will find your own answer, not mine, not from your mama and papa, not from friends, and it will be the right one.

Henry

P.S. Regarding water in the street or other places that might tempt me I give you my word that I will ignore all puddles as per your instructions. I will wait for another rainy day to christen my new boots.

Dear Betsy,

Thank you for the beautiful brooch. It is such a lovely gift, but your presence at my party was more than enough. It was a difficult time for me, as you know, with Anne being gone from us, but, as Henry says, she would have wanted me to celebrate my birthday and so I tried, with as glad a heart as I could summon under the circumstances. Let us get together again soon.

Love,
Mary

P.S. Henry presented me with the perfect gift with which to hold the brooch. It is the most lovely box to hold my keepsakes in, and it means all the more to me because he made it.

Dear Henry,

I have no words adequate enough to thank you. How can I say what it means to have such a beautiful box to hold my keepsakes in, one made by you? All I can say is "thank you", after all, but such an inadequate word has never before existed.

Of course you were right about everything, and though my heart was a bit absent from much of the festivities, your presence at my party helped me cope with the loss of Anne.

A grateful Mary

Dear Mary,

I would like to have given you so much more than a simple wooden box. May you find it a place for your earthly treasures as well as for those of which your dreams are made.

I find my time is taken up these days with much that is of no consequence, but it is good to work, good to sweat a bit to help one's neighbor when called upon. I have been surveying again as well, a lot of work for the town, but some private work as well. I must be leaving soon to meet with some disputing neighbors regarding property lines, boundary lines &c &c.

I find the surveying demands these days a mixed blessing. My labors keep me out of doors rather than in the unwholesome atmosphere of a place of business, but the men who require my services are less than congenial company and I find myself longing for solitude again as though I were starving for it, which I believe I am.

A few more days and I will be free of obligations and find myself restored to sanity once again with a full day of sailing and sauntering.

I hear the clarion call of duty, so I must gather up the gear and meet with my assistant, a good man, but a bit slow. It would benefit me as well as others if I learned to be more patient, though I fear that virtue will be a long time coming.

Henry

P.S. Mary, I rejoice as I feel you returning to us. You have been away too long and we are all the poorer for it.

Dear Henry,

I hope you can put it all aside, this busy-ness, as soon as possible, and find yourself again in the woods, fields and water, but this time not as employee surveyor, but as your true self, where your eyes will not be hired to find old, or create new boundary markers and lot lines.

Will you be able to endure even *my* company, say within the next few days or whenever you are free from further obligations? If so, I am so looking forward to seeing you, as always.

Mary

P.S. I have news that I am longing to share with you, *good* this time!

Dear Mary,

Will you be able to join me for a walk tomorrow in the early afternoon, shall we say around 1:00? I will call for you then unless I hear otherwise. Any other time will be fine if that does not suit you. It will be our last walk for a few days.

The pencil business will require my attention shortly, but tomorrow, I will be most happy to do a ramble with you in field or wood, wherever you choose, or a sail if you prefer.

I *do* need some natural refreshment to restore me without the accompaniment of my surveying tools and I would love your company.

Henry

P.S. Good news, you say, but no further hint? Miss Mary, you are a tease.

Dear Henry,

Bradford and Jane Althorp have surprised us with a
visit today. Well, it is *almost* a surprise but truth be told,
not really at all. I knew that Jane and Bradford were
coming. Jane wrote to me and asked if she and Bradford
could pay us a visit. She hinted very clearly that Bradford
was impatient for another meeting with me, this being
the third one in as many weeks. My desire to see him is
just as strong, but Mama and Papa would never let me see
him alone, so Jane comes with him — which I don't mind
at all, for she has become a dear friend.

I have not said anything to you about Bradford and
me. I think you must disapprove though I don't know
why I feel that you would. I am telling you now because I
cannot bear to keep secrets from you, the man who places
honesty above all other virtues that one can possess.
Forgive me please. I am ashamed of my lack of trust in
you, for I would hear anything you have to say, whether it
is agreeable to me or not.

This is my good news to you. I felt I must say it in
this letter before I see you, but will say more when we are
together.

Oh, Henry, this won't do. I must tell all before I
see you. Bradford and I meet alone and often. Jane visits

Betsy, you remember her, don't you, while Bradford and
I walk and talk, that is all, on my honor, in the Walden
woods because they are close to the village. He hears
it, Henry, he hears it. Music, voices, musical voices.
Whatever it is he hears it and we listen together and it is
if my world has finally come right again. I have been sad
for so long. Perhaps you know why, perhaps not, but it is
all right. I understand.

Mary

Mr. Henry Thoreau,

Your presence is requested here tomorrow for a light luncheon in our garden before we set forth on our walk. Mama has become very fond of you and would enjoy your company at our outdoor table. Berries and a nice little raisin cake will be provided as well, for it is possible that the walk could turn into one of those longer *saunters* which I have come to love as much as you do.

Short walks do not please me as they once did and I have you to thank for showing me that there is much to be gained on these saunters, so much to see, details in the landscape and over our heads in the sky. What I once never paid attention to has now become what I seek.

Let us make a long day of it then and enjoy whatever comes our way. I believe I have heard those sentiments from someone before, "enjoying whatever comes our way." I believe I can say Henry, it was you.

Mary

Well, Miss Mary.

Good news such as yours must be spoken aloud, but of course you understand or you would have let the letter speak for itself.

I believe I could see the colors in your words, with some sparkles thrown in to boot. I do not believe I have ever seen you so bright and *that* is why your words mattered so much, for sparkles and colors do not appear, quite, on paper.

I hope that you will bring your Bradford along on one of our walks so that I might take the measure of the young man, or we can go sailing if he would prefer, maybe a bit of both. I am at your disposal.

Dearest girl. I don't think I need to repeat myself here but I will if it will help you. If it matters at all, I am on your side always. Perhaps you and Bradford know already what you want but if you do, I would advise you not to share it yet. I don't believe your mothers and fathers will be ready to hear what you have to say.

I trust you completely, Mary, your judgment about people, your intuition about them, your divine inner compass that showed itself at such a young age. Just think on it and let it be for now but for this and do not forget it. Never swear to me "on your honor". I will not have

you think that I require a vow from you before you can
be believed, no matter what you do, no matter who you
spend time with alone. Never again, dearest girl.

Henry

Most dear Henry,

Bradford is coming to tea Tuesday next, so you will
meet him then.

Mother has extended an invitation to you as well, so
please do come. You will have every opportunity to "take
the measure of the young man" then.

In the meantime, another walk or sail tomorrow?
We can take a woodland walk first then go for a sail
please, both. I am quite beside myself these days and need
distraction.

Dear Henry, I am counting on you to speak frankly
about any concerns you might have about Bradford. Your
opinion is the one that I value above all others, even more
than that of Mama and Papa. I regret to say that they see
life differently than I do and not only because they are
older. It is just who they are.

Until tomorrow unless you are busy making pencils
or otherwise occupied. I will meet you at our place by
the pond at 1:00. If the time is not convenient do send a
message when there will be a more convenient day and
time for you.

Mary

Dear Mary,

I do not believe I shall find Bradford wanting in any way. You must not take me seriously when I say I must "take the measure" of your young man. Your parents have found it acceptable for him to court their daughter and so shall I as well, though I have no say about it at all but for the fact that you want me to say so.

Much more important is you, how your mind and heart speak to you. You have time to decide what, if anything, this young man will be to you in the future. Enjoy what you have now, when you are together and even those times when you are apart. Though times apart may be the hardest for you to endure, they will be most important, giving you time to reflect upon what you want and need from your life's partner, if indeed, that is the future that you and Bradford are contemplating. Surely it is too soon for that or am I mistaken? That is enough advice from me and a letter is not the proper place to speak of your concerns. Let's talk tomorrow when we meet, what say you to that?

We will fill up as much time as we can when you are free and I am not called upon to do some surveying, though that is a possibility within the next few days. These legs of mine need regular stretching as you know or they are impossible to live with so I must do my best to accommodate them.

Henry

Dear Betsy,

I have committed myself to Bradford. We will be
wed, though no date has been decided upon as yet. I do
love him for so many good reasons. He is quite the best of
me, but I must say this at the risk of confusing you, else I
will be at odds with myself for the rest of my days.

Henry is the measure, the standard by which I
judge all men, Bradford in particular. I have not spoken
to Henry of my feelings for him nor will I for I have
been witness to the occasional way he harshly condemns
himself and his character when speaking of things
personal that have happened in his life, such as the
separation from Mr. Emerson. He does not love me and so
it is and ever will be.

We will always be Mary and Henry, our old selves
with a strong enduring friendship and we will continue
to spend time together walking, talking about life and
magical things and having tea and cakes, and that will
and must be enough for me. I will be Bradford's wife,
gladly so, for he is kind and good and we have much in
common, and I will begin a new life with him, but oh how
I grieve for what could have been.

Dearest Mary,

My heart is breaking for you. I wept when I read your letter. Henry Thoreau is one of the best of men, true, but you have Bradford who loves you and I believe you when you say you love him as well, despite the conflicted feelings you have for Mr. Thoreau.

Give yourself completely to Bradford, Mary, mind, body, heart and soul, else you will have a marriage in name only and you and Bradford will be husband and wife in name only as well. You cannot want to live your life that way, as so many, too many marriages do, lives and futures shattered. Henry is unavailable, but you know that, so I need not say more. Count your blessings then, for you have won Bradford Althorp's heart. Hold it, cherish it. Henry would want you to.

Love,
Betsy

Dear Henry,

I have had time to myself for a number of days. But for assisting mother or Fanny with marketing or some such thing, my time has been my own. I have gotten better acquainted with our flower garden as well as with some of the less frequented roads to the village, the ones that we take most often.

Taking your advice, which I almost always do, I have reflected, contemplated, thought, dreamed awake and asleep and come to the conclusion that I believe I love Bradford. I cannot tell you how I know it for there are no words for such feelings, just that I do, but I will try to explain. He is the music that I hear in the woods, he is the voice that whispers to me as I walk along those paths where I believe no one goes anymore but you and me. He is the hand that steadies me when I falter, the one who helps me to my feet when I fall. He *believes* not only in the uncommon world that you and I know, but in the beauty of the overlooked and undervalued things that are taken for granted, the so-called common things that you and I see every moment we spend together.

When we were together last, our talk, with your clarity and lack of sentimentality, helped clarify my feelings and for that I thank you, dear friend, and no it is not too soon to believe in a future with Bradford.

Dear Miss Bright,

You have made the case. There is nothing more I can say about you and Bradford that you have not already said to yourself. You have done what was required, not by any prompting on my part, but with your own common sense, balancing the stirrings of your loving and tender heart and the responses that come from those quiet reflections that you spoke of, where your thoughts go, asking and answering your own questions, all or most as may be in the affirmative for Bradford Althorp as your future husband. I have already given you my best thoughts such as they are.

Will you be available for a light luncheon day after tomorrow? What do you say to a picnic at Fairhaven Hill? An overstuffed basket will be provided, thanks to the chief cook and her staff of one from the Thoreau kitchen. It is your day so I await your pleasure. Will a sail or walk suit after we eat? You choose. Oh Mary, my dearest girl.

Dear Channing,

Be that bad boy if you must. I will love you no less
for I know *your* heart as impenetrable as mine and no less
troubled, but fine and good despite your best efforts to
make it seem otherwise.

All has been put to rest and I am thankful for it
but wistfully so. Let us put it to rest as well, I must, with
no questions on your part and no answers on mine. You
know what I am saying without me spelling it out for you.
And end to it then, Ellery, I beg you.

Thoreau

Dear Thoreau,

Regarding the contents of your letter, you have my word.

I have often pondered why we get on as well as we do. Is it because, think you, that you carry the same dark impulses inside you that I do, the difference being that I act on mine where you cover yours up with those fine inner feelings and good intentions, because you are afraid of what you might do if you break the seal on that inner door that holds you in check? Or is it the reverse, that I have the purity of soul, mind and heart that you do and it is those interior ties we share that bind us together, one to the other? Could you even tolerate, let alone love me as your friend if that were not true?

Hidden within those unfathomable depths of yours, rarely seeing the light of day are those rare moments where you are compelled to reveal yourself, with the doubts and fears and anxieties that make you human, that make you one of us, like now, a man conflicted and in pain.

You are an enigma, Thoreau, and I know that you will remain so by choice so I will let the rhetorical questions remain as they are, rhetorical, unanswered and unanswerable. But we will be friends to the last, my enigmatic friend, with ties that bind whether of the dark or of the light. Who will ever be able to understand us, for we often cannot understand each other?

Yours truly,
Channing

Dear Henry,

I hear from Bradford that you and he are undertaking a trip to Worcester to meet with your friend Mr. Blake, and then on to Mt. Monadnock for a few days. From your description of Mr. Blake he sounds most congenial and a potential good new friend for Bradford. Obviously you are in agreement or you would not have proposed a meeting and a few days spent in each others' company.

This will be good for B. He is as ill-tempered as I have been of late. Unpardonable, but there it is, with no excuses, except that we seem to be playing a "waiting game" of sorts. All will be sorted out soon, I hope, when we reveal our future plans to the mamas and papas. I fear I will hear that I am too young and that Bradford cannot possibly support a wife when he becomes a student in medical school, which will be in a few short weeks. I believe I mentioned his future plans to you, did I not? You have been uncharacteristically silent on this subject. I would know why, Mr. Thoreau.

Mary

Most Dear Mary,

You want to know why I haven't spoken of your age and Bradford's studies and how they will be used to dissuade you from too early a marriage. A very simple answer. You will hear enough about that from the "mamas and papas," I expect. You don't need me to add to their objections. You know how I feel. We have talked often and exchanged letters, but about *this* subject which may arouse parental disapproval I have no voice, Mary. I am friend only, no relation. My opinions are irrelevant. Listen kindly, patiently to them as I know you will without my counsel.

Henry

Dear Mary,

I must get back to the pencil business for the time being. Bradford and Blake hit it off splendidly. It was a happy reward for me to see the beginnings of a new friendship unfold between two such worthy men. They entertained each other far into the night with stories of mutual interest, young doctor-to-be and minister turned teacher, while I occupied myself by star-gazing and walking a bit under a night sky, with a full moon in bloom to light my way.

It was glorious, and so I have returned to the work that awaits me in a better frame of mind than when I left. I can only hope that my good intentions to keep that positive frame of mind will last until the call to dinner, so I will keep a tight rein on the memory of the stars and moon, lest the drudgery of pencil making drive them from my thoughts.

Henry

P.S. Maybe in a week or so we can have that saunter, a "sail and cakes day." I'll let you know when I can be more specific about time.

Most dear friend,

Henry, it has happened. Last evening after dining we all gathered in the parlor, mamas, papas, and of course Bradford and myself to speak frankly about our marriage, concerns, objections, all of it, and after an amiable discussion, with no tempers lost, (a miracle if I do say so) Papa gave his consent and blessing and Mrs. Althorp, soon to be Mother Althorp embraced me and called me her dear daughter!

I confess I may have cheated a bit by reminding my own mama of her age when she married, a young girl just turned seventeen, so she had but a weak protest to make about our plans to wed the day after my seventeenth birthday which will be in a month's time. And Papa remained completely silent the entire time, for he knew I had won the argument. It will feel like a lifetime, but I will be a good patient girl and count the days with not a word of complaint from my lips.

I am inviting you to come Thursday next for a party to celebrate B's and my engagement. Please let nothing prevent you from attending. You know how I count on your presence there.

Mary

P.S. The party will be small, just close friends and family, some of whom you already know. If you would like, bring your friend Mr. Channing. You speak of him often and I would very much like to meet him.

Dear Mary,

I always speak plainly as you know, but I will do my best to tread lightly here, for this is a subject which really concerns only you and Bradford. I hope that I do not risk unraveling the fine and tender threads of our friendship but I believe that they are strong and will hold. Your news was not unexpected, but still I rejoice with you both, for I know that your hearts were set on this happy outcome. I am the least qualified to say anything at all about marriage, therefore let my thoughts live or die according to their merits if they have any. Do please forgive if I trespass into unfamiliar and personal territory with these few words.

You will have a busy household and you will be the head of all domestic concerns, from the kitchen to the upper and lower chambers, even if you have hired help. Your husband will require attention from you, as you will from him, in all ways relating to the heart and beyond, things that only lovers can and should speak of.

I have seen you grow from a lovely child to an even more lovely young woman, one who loves life with a fervor and passion rarely seen in one so young, who has not outgrown her ability to see and hear the marvels that reside in every nook and cranny of wood and field, aye, and water, too, and everywhere you look.

Bring all of these gifts, dear Mary, so many that you have, to your future life. I have not been so fortunate, for my love was lost to me as you know, but I will speak no more about that. You and Bradford have your own story and I hope to be privileged enough to see where it takes you, and what wonders unfold for you in the weeks, months and years to come.

Nothing will keep me from attending your engagement party. Ellery Channing is out of the country at present and I'm unsure when he will return, but I thank you on his behalf for the invitation. I am at a loss as to know how to close this letter, so just this and no more. I love you both.

Henry

Dear Henry,

I must confess that I felt distressed when first I read your letter, that you could wonder or doubt that I would have taken offense at any words you expressed so thoughtfully and with so much care. Surely as you said, the threads of friendship that bind us together are strong and will withstand anything.

Mary, with much love to her Henry

P.S. I shared the letter with Bradford and he was deeply touched. I believe you have not only a friend but a new brother as well.

Mary,

Dear girl, where have you gone? You haven't answered my last two letters. I can only conclude that you have good reasons for not responding. But I must hear from you, so I write again with renewed hopes that you will answer.

Please may I call on you? I have cream and a basket of fresh berries from a kind neighbor to coax you, a small offering but one that I hope will find favor so that I may see you and be assured that you are all right.

Henry

I fear that I have offended you. If I have done so please forgive.

Dear Henry,

Forgive you? It is I who must be forgiven for worrying you by my indefensible disregard of your feelings.

Everything has gone wrong, Henry, and I am quite beside myself and so angry with Bradford. He has decided with his parents wholehearted support to study abroad for a year. He is leaving in less than a week. I do not know what I shall do. Here we are, our betrothal announced at our engagement party and he is off to Europe. I certainly cannot wait for years to pass before we marry while he is studying in Europe. He thinks that having more education will be beneficial for his future medical practice and now he wants to become a surgeon.I guess just a plain simple doctor is not good enough for him.

I can see absolutely no reason why he cannot stay here and study in New York or Boston.

I am completely out of sorts so you must forgive this letter. He is leaving in less than a week, believing that I entirely support this decision. No I do not support it, but I bite my tongue lest I say something that I will later regret.

Your penitent friend

P.S. Please let us walk soon, a long one. Mama will be relieved to get rid of me for a few hours. I feel like it will take days to get me sorted out again.

Dear Girl,

You are pardoned, forgiven and absolved if that is what it takes to make you feel better. Take me up on my offer to meet with you, berries and fresh cream in hand or not to put too fine a point on it, in basket, and we will spend as much time as you wish, until you can no longer tolerate my company. We can converse while sailing or walking or be still and say nothing at all. It is your call and I will follow your lead.

Henry

P.S. I have some repair work on a fence to attend to, but will be free after tomorrow.. Send a messenger with day and time or just whistle and I will come a-running.

Dear Mary,

Both of us seemed to avoid talking about what must
have been foremost in your mind when last we met, so let
me do so now.

I understand how disappointed you are, but permit
me to be an advocate for Bradford. This is his chance to
fulfill a dream, one that he talked about it at length when
we camped at Mt. Monadnock. Perhaps he has already
shared what I will relate to you. But I doubt that you have
heard his story else you would not have expressed such
distress in your letter to me.

Bradford has written to me, as troubled as *you* are,
for he knows how his new plans have upset you and he
has asked me to speak to you on his behalf which I agreed
to do, Mary, caring for you both as I do.

As we sat around the fire one night on that trip,
Blake and Bradford and I, we spoke of many things
until at length the subject came round to our hopes and
aspirations, our goals in the present and for the future,
even dreams that may or may not have a chance of being
realized in our lifetimes. Bradford spoke of being a lad of
twelve, watching the old doctor that tended to his family
and his neighbors for he was allowed to accompany him
occasionally as he made his rounds. He believed, even at

that young age, that something was amiss, that the cares and concerns of patients could be better served by higher education and so resolved that he would be that missing piece when he was older, able to pursue his educational goals and he is now ready to fulfill that promise that he made to himself as a boy.

London, England seems to be the place for him Mary, especially with his new goal to become a surgeon, and not just a family doctor. Please do not mistake these words to you. I take no sides here. I have not forgotten you and your feelings, beyond the disappointment of having him gone for so many months. You are resilient Mary and not the only one whose dreams have had to be deferred. Think not on what you are losing temporarily but what will come to you when Bradford has completed his studies and is a physician surgeon. Let his dreams become yours for now and have no doubt that yours, whatever they are or will be, will become his.

I will be delighted to distract you with your favorite activities, maybe even attending a gathering with your friends if you are courageous enough to invite me. Maybe someone else can see to that, someone more congenial than the curmudgeon who is penning this letter. Otherwise, I am at your disposal for sailing, sauntering, even a picnic or two where we can relax and look for hidden treasures in some out of the way places that we have never discovered before. I have no doubt that there are many just waiting for us to find them out. Please do not turn away from family and friends who love you. There is much to be said for tenderhearted company when one is in need.

Dear Henry,

I love everyone who has put up with me these last weeks. I will be glad of your company whenever you are free to call on me and it matters not what we do.

I just want to be with you.

Mary

P.S. You said everything I needed to hear, curmudgeon most dear.

Dear Henry,

I have no words to express my joy, thanks to Mama and Papa. They have consented to let me visit Bradford in England! For a whole month! I do not believe they could bear one more day of me in my present state of mind so they are sending me away. James will escort me to London, then will return to the farm where he is living now with our cousin and uncle, and Bradford will come home with me at month's end. He has taken some weeks off from his studies to visit his family, so it works out perfectly for both of us.

I must see you before I leave, which will be within a week, barely enough time to organize everything. I must make some purchases, visit the dressmaker, so many things to do.

Let's agree on a time right now. I will make myself available with some short notice from you. I hope that there are no projects you are engaged in that will keep you from a good long saunter before I leave. Please find time for something even if it has to be a walk around the garden.

Mary

My dear Mary,

This is what was needed to make you smile again and put some color back in your cheeks. What an opportunity for you to see new and wonderful things, a completely different way for you to experience the world, not forgetting the main reason for your journey of course, which is to see Bradford.

Drink it all in, the sights, the sounds, colors, flavors, yes, flavors of what life in London has to offer her American cousin. Let all of your senses come completely to life and you will see what I mean. Enjoy it all, then come back with stories to share so that your family can see it all through your eyes.

I look forward to hearing Bradford's account of London as well. He will have absorbed some of the taste and customs of his temporary home and I expect that I will see some changes from the man he was before he left for England to the man he has become.

Your father will let me know the date of your return so that I will be free to go with him and your mother to welcome you home.

Henry

Dear Henry,

Can you not spend some time with your wayward friend, even a short walk or small luncheon here before I begin the necessary but tedious preparations for my journey? I have not received a word from you.

I will await your reply, but do not let too much time go by, else I will be overwhelmed with tasks small and large that must be attended to.

Mary

Dear Mary,

I can see you tomorrow afternoon but, alas, no luncheon of any size at all for I will be planting a few dozen saplings for Mr. Emerson. I should be through before 3:00 if someone can keep me informed of the time and if I have no interruptions. If that time is acceptable, I will call for you then.

We will make the most of our walk if we put our minds and hearts into the enjoyment of it and put other concerns aside.

Do not fret, I will have you home again with time to spare as you continue the preparations for your trip. Wayward? Yes. And you must always remain so.

Henry

P.S. Forgive my delay in responding to your letter. I was indisposed, but all is well now.

Dear Henry,

Luncheon is not important. I find that I am becoming quite anxious about my voyage. There is so much to do and I feel dreadfully unprepared. Seeing you even briefly is the best thing that will happen to me today. If we go to our place in the woods will we still hear music? Say yes and I will believe again. I have been too long away. I will be ready whenever you come for me.

Mary

My dear Mary,

I feel I must answer this by messenger before I see you. You ask if our friends make music still? Yes, I can attest to it, for I go to the woods often to refresh myself after a day that has come down hard on me. Would that more townsmen and women could have the experience as well instead of attending to the hollow speech of the marketplace or barroom or from the pulpit of a Sunday morning. Lives might be changed at once and for the better if they could employ their celestial senses instead putting attention to the trivialities of their empty minds.

We will make the most of the short time together. It is what we put into it that counts, not the movement of the minutes and hours on the face of the steeple clock. I look forward to visiting our friends with you. It *has* been a long while since we have sought their company together, too long. Be at peace, Mary. All will be well.

Henry

Most dear Henry,

There is no time for you to answer, so I am sending this by messenger simply to say a few words before I leave for England.

If I have not thanked you for your tender care and efforts to cheer me over the last few weeks, I want to now, with many apologies for not having done it sooner. I can imagine you turning your face from me in embarrassment if I would speak these next words to you personally, so I will say what comes next in this brief note rather than in conversation.

You are a good man, kind and tender with a loving heart. Do take care of yourself, saunter, sail, and take a tea cake to our friends in the wood. I will miss it all despite the joys and pleasures of visiting a new country. If you could stand the long journey I would ask you to accompany me to see Bradford, but I know that you and the ocean are barely on speaking terms and so we will have a good long saunter when I return instead. Concord is my home as much as it is yours and I will be counting the days until I am back with you, family and friends again, this time not alone but with Bradford.

Mary

P.S. Bradford mentioned in his last letter that he was eager to see you again and become reacquainted with Mr. Blake. I think he is hoping for another expedition including hiking, climbing and whatever else can be mutually agreed upon, as long as it is risky.

Dear Henry,

I have been feted by my family, friends and Bradford's family until I am quite exhausted, as lovely as it has been, at least at first, to be the subject of so much attention. I fear, alas, that my trip to London has been reduced to simply a recitation of the latest fashions, the museums, the mansions on Belgrave Square and other grand addresses, even to the livery that the butlers and footmen and ladies maids and valets are required to wear. I have never heard of such nonsense and it pains me to have to recite it.

Bradford is as tired of it as I am, but he is a dutiful son so he must put up with it longer than I, for his family is much larger than mine.

Please take me on a jaunt somewhere where I can feel the wind in my hair again and feel the sun on my cheek. When Bradford can free himself from family obligations he will be able to join us, but this first walk must be ours.

Mary

P.S. Forgive my writing only a short note or two while in London. I'll make up for it when we get

together again with some topics that would be of
interest only to you.

Dear Mary,

Name the day and time and I will come to fetch you and a-sauntering we will go, but first it must be tea and cakes at the house.

Mother and Sophia have missed you almost as much as I, and I fear will ask you to recount those same tiresome details of the latest fashions in London and gossip that you have already been forced to relate to family and friends. I apologize on their behalf, but one more recounting of your London adventures will not go unrewarded. Perhaps extra cakes and tea, which I will benefit from as well.

I continually strive for those qualities of character that you see in me, Mary, but despite my best efforts I always seem to miss the mark, qualities that my brother John embodied effortlessly. What little bit of grace in my conduct I have acquired over the years is due entirely to my modeling myself after him. But I thank you, dearest girl, for your kind words.

Henry

Dearest Henry,

I am sending Fanny to your house with a basket
of eggs and some vegetables from our garden with my
deepest thanks and gratitude for the wonderful welcome
home I received from your mother and Sophia. I love
them too as part of my own family and was so happy to
see them again and looking so well. I actually enjoyed
recounting news about my brief trip to London just to
witness their delight.

And now Henry, this is news for you! I cannot wait
to tell you in person. There is a surgeon who has recently
opened a school with two other physicians to teach men
like Bradford who wish to expand their knowledge of the
arts of medicine specializing in surgery.

This doctor, I believe his name is Joseph Thurgood,
has associates in London and Vienna and one of
Bradford's professors in London contacted Dr. Thurgood
about Bradford and asked if he would accept him as a
student, giving details about what an excellent student
B. is and what a credit he would be to the school. This is
the best plan, for B. has spoken to me about Dr. Thurgood,
whose reputation is very well known all over the world
and how he would love to take instruction from him. And
now this very man is right here in Boston.

Henry, I fear I am rambling. What an unforeseen and welcome turn of events.

Mary

Most dear Mary,

May I call on you within the next day or two? It is important to hear your happy news in person. I have not shared anything with Mother and Sophia. It is your good news to tell.

Mother says she will put together a repast fit for a king, a queen in this case. Expect some very good eating and lots of questions from Sophia. I suspect they know something is up but they are not letting on, hoping I will drop a hint.

Henry

P.S. Please give my best to Bradford.

Mr. Bradford Althorp,

The excursion to Mt. Wachusett was certainly a surprise. There were some very shrewd maneuverings on the part of Mr. Thoreau that enabled him to pull this trip off without a hint to anyone.

It has been whispered about that Mr. Althorp's fiance Mary Bright was a bit miffed that she was not told about this excursion, but that is simply kitchen gossip and should be ignored.

The fact is Miss Bright is extending an invitation to both Mr. Althorp and Mr. Thoreau to join her for a casual tea, perhaps a picnic weather permitting with sandwiches and favorite cakes made by her own hand, the time and place to be determined, depending upon Mr. Thoreau's work schedule and Mr. Althorp's familial responsibilities.

An acceptance or decline of the invitation is expected and should be sent by post to Miss Mary Bright. The address is known to both parties.

Very truly yours.

Dear Henry,

Thank heavens B. you, and Mr. Blake have returned from Mt. Wachusett without incident. I had horrible images in my mind of someone falling from treacherous slopes or wild animals setting upon you while slumbering beneath benign and starry skies completely unaware of the peril you were in. I know how indifferent you are to calamity when you set your mind upon other things that are more important to you, like climbing and botanizing.

I assume B. has told you of my invitation to a picnic. Do say you will join us. I leave the time and place of our gathering in your hands. Send a message and Bradford and I will meet you there.

Mary

Dear Mary,

I am sorry that you were anxious about the trip. I have been to that mountain before and Bradford was in good, very capable hands. Not even a rainy day and night could dampen his enthusiasm.

Do please have enough confidence in me now to have a light heart and easy mind when and if Bradford and I decide to venture forth on another long outing. I have it in my mind to invite either Blake or Channing to accompany us in the future. Blake and Bradford are already fast friends and Channing would be a good addition, good but unpredictable which makes time spent with him all the more interesting.

What do you say to a picnic today at Walden pond at the site where my house once stood? I will provide cider and a blanket to sit upon and the pond will give us water. How is 1:00 for a time? Come to my house and we can set off from there, giving mother and Sophia a chance to meet Bradford. Let's make it around 12:30 if that is not too early.

Henry

I must add this to what I have already said. Forgive

please my insensitivity. Your concern for us was understandable. I am used to being accountable only to myself with no wife or beloved to be responsible to or for, who might consider my adventures ill-advised and reckless. I assure you Mary that I would never put my friends in harm's way. Blake, Channing and others who have taken treks and overnight outings with me are fine travelers who enjoy roughing it and Bradford can hold his own with any of them.

Henry

Most dear Curmudgeonly, (you *were* rather you know,
though you did ask my forgiveness which of course you
have without asking for it)

The picnic was divine, the food delicious, the sail
afterwards thrilling, the company beyond compare. Your
mother and Sophia were their hospitable and lovely selves
and quite enchanted B. I daresay he would like to move to
your house and stay there for as long as you would have
him.

I am losing him to Boston for a while where he will
begin his studies with Professor Thurgood but that is so
much more agreeable than watching him sail away on
a ship bound for England. He will return to Concord at
week's end where hopefully we will have some private
moments if his family does not make too many demands
on his time.

Do you have an idle hour or two where you might
be free for a saunter? Let me know forthwith so that I can
make other plans if you are unavailable.

Mary

P.S. *Forthwith.* Does that sound pretentious?

Dear Miss Pretentious,

I will be unable to accompany you *forthwith* so it will have to be *by and by* due to an uncommon amount of work that has been recently thrust upon me. I will be quite overloaded for almost a fortnight but will try to be available to accompany you on the 30th to do whatever you fancy or to go wherever you will.

Please inform me, Miss P., by post, on foot, or by carriage, whatever suits you and if you will be available on that day, being the aforementioned 30th of the month. I leave the time to you, the earlier the better. As you know, I tend to be out of sorts when working overlong in the company of others some of whom I can barely tolerate, but when next we meet I shall have recovered myself sufficiently and I hope you will find me thoroughly, maybe even unbearably, agreeable.

Very truly curmudgeonly yours,
Henry

Dear Mr. Curmudgeon,

I will be ready at 2:00 on the 30th for you to call upon when I will be looking forward to a good long walk. We must have our tea and cakes first to fortify ourselves for I daresay it will be a very long one if I read your letter correctly. I do believe you will be in need of one.

My own walks have consisted of strolls around the garden and to the market, hardly worth the description of *walk* at all. It seems we are both in serious need of reacquainting ourselves with the woods and fields.

Mary — also occasionally known as Miss Pretentious but only to those who love her best and so put up with her nonsense.

Dear Betsy,

Bradford and I have set a date for the wedding. You are the first to know. Henry has not been told yet, for I asked Bradford if I could give him the good news myself.

You must stand with me at the altar along with Jane, of course. Bradford intends to ask Henry to be his best man and I will not be able to do this, facing him standing next to Bradford if you are not there as my friend and support. I will give you more of the details in a day or two, but I must tell Henry. So much is happening all at once. I must tell him now before more time goes by and I am completely lost in the frivolous details of the preparations.

Mary

My dear friend Mary,

I will be honored to stand with you on your wedding
day. I would have been sorely disappointed had you not
asked me, but, I confess, being as close as we are I had
half expected it. I daresay you will not be distressed at
Henry's presence there. I predict that you and Bradford
will have eyes only for each other. Just wait and you will
see that I am right.

I long to go shopping with you, for there will be
things I need to purchase to make myself worthy of being
your bridesmaid, but I suppose that is a mother's duty to
attend to her daughter's trousseau and a third party, even
a friend, would not be welcome at such a time. Anyway
dear, do not fret. All will come out right, you will see. It
would be grand if we could get together, just the two of us
before your big day. Let me know and we will make plans,
soon, because time is running short.

Adieu,
Betsy

Most dear Henry,

Bradford and I have set a date to be wed. I had to send this letter to give you the news in case too much time passes before we can meet.

How could time pass so quickly and yet be so agonizingly slow? Where has my childhood gone, Henry? My dolls are all put away and I see things on my dressing table that belong to a woman, and yet, I fear, I am not quite that woman that I need to be, the one that will be wife and someday a mother. I think I must fail and be so much less than Bradford expects me to be or deserves. I think that I am not alone with misgivings such as these, that all of us who are soon to become wives feel as I do — but that is no consolation to me.

Mother has counseled me, of course, about my wifely duties, about everything I must do to make my husband happy and content, to make him eager to return to me after a long day of tending to his patients.

What about *me*, Henry? What about what I will need to be happy and content? Why do mothers never talk to their daughters about finding what things will make *them* happy, to give them the inner peace they need to maintain that comfortable home, to find creative and satisfying ways to express themselves?

How can a husband be truly happy if he has a
discontented wife?

Bradford is the kind of man whom I know suits my
wayward temperament, of which, more than anyone,
you are aware. But we are not yet together every day and
every night. I will most assuredly not be the obedient wife
that most men expect their wives to be, though I will try
to be reasonable and not fixed in my opinions without
giving his thoughts just consideration.

Henry, I am all in a muddle. You can see from this
letter than I move from one thought to another.

I believe I need a long saunter and conversation with
you, dear Henry, rather than hearing from you by post.

I can see you *anytime*, the sooner the better.

A very anxious Mary

Most dear girl,

Since you have not proposed a specific time I say
tomorrow for luncheon at my house, 12:00, where you will
be fussed over by sister Sophia, Mother, aunts and even
Uncle Charles, for he is visiting at present. He might even
swallow his nose for you with little or no prompting, a
feat that I tried many times without success when I was
a youngster and, I confess, as late as yesterday evening.
Unsuccessful as usual, though the family cheered me
on with a great deal of enthusiasm. Then we will take
ourselves off on either a walk, a sail, or a combination
of both if you wish for as long as you can endure my
company. Please try to get permission to spend some of
the evening hours with us as well, with a bit of supper to
boot before I see you home. We might even be blessed by
the serenade of a thrush or a whippoorwill as they bid
farewell to the day and signal the arrival of the evening
hours with their sweet songs.

Now to address your news. I will say something
now, but let us talk about it tomorrow as well if I do
not answer all of your concerns here. I am at your
disposal always, at any time but you already know
that. I do not know the importance of what I have to
say to you. I express myself awkwardly when speaking

of personal, even intimate, issues such as this, but I will give it my best.

I will dispense with the usual hackneyed expressions that most people use when given news such as yours, a wedding, a betrothal, &c so I will begin this way.

You and Bradford are well matched in an unusual way that perhaps is overlooked by friends and family, maybe even by yourselves. I watch you together and I hear your words when you are apart, speaking of each other. I see where there is great strength in him and when you have need of it, he will not fail to lift you up. I see it in his eyes, I hear it in his voice. Where there is weakness in him, I see him rally with the strength that you give him to lean upon, to help him recover and overcome the most difficult challenges, because of your love and faith in him. This is what I see, this is what I believe about you and Bradford and there is much more that I am not privy to, that only you and he can know about each other.

You, Mary, are best able to meet your own needs in your marriage, apart from being Bradford's wife. Have you not always been able to find the things in life that fill you with joy and contentment, that feed your insatiable curiosity and the delightful willfulness that you refuse to suppress, a quality that makes you so unique among women? I see those qualities that you share with only a few of those women I know, my Mother and the love who lives far from me are two of them. You will not lose these wondrous qualities, anymore than you can change your eyes from brown to blue. Marriage for a woman like you will only bring out your best, you can count on it.

I will stop now, for I fear my words will begin to run into one another and lose their heart and meaning and whatever significance they might have for you, like one of those musty old preachers who put people to sleep in their pews of a wasted Sunday morning.

Luncheon tomorrow at 12:00? Uncle Charles is no match for you. You will charm him as easily as you have delighted the entire Thoreau family, then you and I will do whatever you wish.

Dear Henry,

I am so looking forward to your company and the hospitality of your wonderful family.

Papa has given his consent to letting me spend the evening with you and your family, but requests that you have me home at 8:00.

Henry, I feel a bit uncomfortable about your Uncle Charles. He sounds quite formidable from your description. Will you speak to him before we meet? I would not want to give him the impression that I feel awkward around him, but I do believe I will.

Mary

Most dear Mary,

My uncle is quite harmless, I assure you. As outrageous as he is, and I confess that is indeed true, he is a gentleman through and through. He would not for a minute distress you by saying or doing something to offend your sensibilities. I will ask him to refrain from swallowing his nose or standing on his head in your company, but you might regret it later as a missed opportunity if you do not let him perform for you. We Thoreaus are quite used to his antics and have decided to put up with him for he is dear, but I will have a word with him on your behalf if you wish it.

Henry

Most Dear Mary,

You have quite charmed Uncle Charles, but that was no surprise to me and you brought out his best which is there in abundance when he is of a mind to reveal it. I hope you know that you are another sister to Sophia and daughter to my mother as if you were their own.

If you doubted what I said to you on our walk yesterday or need further reassurance I will say it again on paper, this being a long postscript, perhaps, added to my previous letter. Read it until the ink fades and there is nothing left to see, until the voice in your head is quieted. Then let your heart be heard, for that is where true wisdom resides.

You are the love Bradford has been seeking, else he would not have offered himself up to you as he has done, to be a friend, lover, husband.

Speak to Bradford as openly and honestly as you have spoken to me. Who is more important to hear your thoughts and concerns if not the man you are soon to wed? Please, Mary. Do not be afraid to open yourself up to him, else after you are wed you may find it easy to put off a conversation that could prevent a serious misunderstanding.

Henry

Very dear Henry,

I take the words you wrote me to heart for I know the wise man from whom they came. After speaking to you and taking the advice from your letter I spoke to Bradford. You were right, of course, and he shared some concerns of his with me as well, about the responsibilities he will be assuming, being a medical student while caring for a new wife and meeting her needs. And there is where our concerns became identical, for I will have a husband whose needs must be met as well.

Henry, I have learned so much from you. Without knowing you all of these years and being so fortunate to receive so much important counsel this conversation between Bradford and myself would never have taken place. I am going to stop now or I will become gushy and that would not do, would it?

Mother and I are going to Boston for a quick visit to some friends who will be attending the wedding and to do some shopping. I will let you know when we return because I will definitely be in need of some quiet time with the man whom I love second best in the world.

Mary

Dear Henry,

We are returning tomorrow afternoon from Boston. What a whirlwind of unnecessary activity! Everyone is in a dither about one thing or another and I am fairly worn out with shopping and too much conversation.

Bradford will be returning to Concord with me where hopefully things will quiet down a bit. We had a few precious hours together between plans with friends and my appointments with dressmakers in Boston, but I long for the peace of the wonderful place that I call home.

I will need a day of rest when I return and will be seeing Bradford off to Boston again too soon, but then let us find some quiet time together. I long for our woodland walks and to hear again from Those Who Are and from you.

Mary

Dear Mary,

May I call for you in two days time for a picnic lunch provided by Mother. She is going to make your favorite snack cakes again, one from a recipe provided by you I believe, and will also include some cold chicken and fruit to top it off.

I will be ready for an excursion as well, being tied to pencil making most of the time you were gone. I am itching for a long walk with you and a lot of good conversation.

Henry

Dear Henry,

I trust that you will permit me to address you
with this letter heading rather than the conventional
"Thoreau"? I would feel a fool calling you anything but
Henry, given our admittedly short, but most agreeable
connection.

I am a bit unsure how to proceed with this request,
but getting right to it is the best way and surely what you
would prefer.

I lost my brother Emery when I was but thirteen
years old. He is not here, but I ask you, in his name, to
stand next to me at the altar when I take Mary for my
wife. I need you there, as my truest friend, and as Mary's
best and dearest, so I ask this for her sake as well.

I realize what I am asking of you and I do not
underestimate the difficulty you might have making
this decision. I would hear from you in person if possible
rather than by post, at your earliest convenience. I am
prepared to be disappointed, but my regard for you will
not be altered in the slightest if you turn me down.

Yours,
Bradford

My dear friend Bradford,

Thank you for the "Henry" in place of the commonly used "Thoreau" in your opening greeting. As you can see, I have followed suit, so it is decided. Bradford and Henry it shall be, if there shall be any correspondence between us in the future. I'm afraid my time is not my own for the next few days, so I must answer you in this less than satisfactory way, by letter.

The request you have made of me to be your best man, I believe it is called. Aye, that is the problem right there, friend, "the best man." I would not call myself so even when I am at my most congenial and agreeable.

I ask you to reconsider, for I have a fragile truce with the church as it stands, and fear that anything out of the ordinary, such as my appearing suddenly within its four walls might send it tumbling about our ears. But if you are determined to risk it, I guess I am as well. It will be my honor to be your man, best or not, on your wedding day.

Yours,
Henry

Dearest Henry,

I must tell you about the strangest dream I had last night. Bradford was in it, and you, though I didn't actually see you. Bradford was saying something to me, quite preposterous, something about the wedding and his best man. He said, let me see if I can get this right as I am relating it to you, that he has asked you to be the best man at our wedding and you *agreed*. I awoke, believing that surely that I was suffering from some kind of nervous indisposition. There is no other way to explain it.

When next I see you we will have a good laugh about it over tea and cakes, which will hopefully be soon.

Mary

Dear Miss Bright, still,

To prove to you that you were not dreaming please accompany me two days hence to my tailor's shop where I am expected for a fitting of a new frock coat. Yes, I am going to be the best man at a wedding within the next fortnight and I feel, because of my very special feelings for the bride and groom, that I should present as respectable an appearance as possible. There is no help for it but that I will try my best, given the poor material there is to work with. Alas, there is nothing I can do about that.

Unless I hear otherwise I shall call for you on Wednesday at 2:00 in the afternoon where I will treat you to tea and cakes after the business is concluded at the aforementioned tailor's.

Yours,
Henry David Thoreau

P.S. Why should I ask you to accompany me, you might very well ask? Because, as much as I care for you and Bradford I fear I might bolt if you do not. Such a large congregation and in such a place sets my teeth on edge.

Dear Mr. Thoreau,

Your invitation to accompany you to your tailor proved I was not dreaming so I thank you for that reassurance, that I had not lost my senses. You *do* cut quite a dashing figure. When Betsy sees you in your new coat with that plum-colored velvet collar I believe she will be quite determined to pursue you. No amount of protest on your part will change that, for she is as willful as I, maybe moreso. I have heard her sing your praises to the skies more than once, so be on your guard lest you become ensnared.

Soon to be Mrs.Bradford Althorp who will see to it that you do not bolt, though I understand why you might be tempted.

My dear Mary,

Betsy is a charming young woman. She will be spoken for soon enough. Since making her acquaintance the few times I have seen her in your company at gatherings which I have attended I have been aware of at least two young men who appear to be vying for her attention. Perhaps one of them will catch her eye and consider himself blessed for the chance to court her.

Henry

Dear Henry,

Bradford is spending all his time with his large family. They are claiming all of his attention before the wedding, as if they will never see him again once we are wed.

Thank heavens I have you, for I feel if I do not get away from *my* family I will surely suffocate and B. will be standing with only you for company at the altar.

Please let me know when you can come and take me away for a very long sail, saunter, whatever suits you. I am indifferent, for both have charms enough to soothe me, but I must see our Friends before I wed. You know of whom I speak.

Anytime, dear Henry, but soon.

Mary

P.S. I have something to say to you. I must be with you in our place else I will not be able to tell it.

Dearest girl,

I will call on you this afternoon. Will you be ready within the hour? Send a note back and upon receiving it I will set forth immediately or whenever a time is more agreeable to you.

I would not want the word to circulate among our worthy townsmen that I would be indifferent to the pleas of a damsel in distress. My reputation might suffer and as things are, based on the opinion of said townsmen, there is not much of it left intact so I suppose I must preserve what is left. What there is, I save for you and your predicament.

Henry

My dear Mary,

We have laughed and wept together many times
over the years, have we not, as I reminded you in a recent
letter. We have shared feelings in those ways which are
far more eloquent than mere words. I am reminded of the
music language of our friends who speak with wordless
communication, as we use our tears and laughter to
express *our* deepest feelings.

Why am I saying these things? Because I understand
why Bradford has changed his mind and feels that
London serves his needs better than remaining in
Boston to continue his studies. It is not necessary for
you to defend his decision or to apologize for it. He has
made this decision based on much careful thought and
reflection, I am sure.

Let it be recorded here, to be read by you as many
times as need be. Will I miss you when you move to London?
Yes. Do I forgive you for waiting so long to tell me about
your plans? Yes, but forgiveness has no place here for it is
irrelevant. That is why I said what I did at the beginning
of this letter, to remind you of the quality and depth upon
which our friendship is built. I am moving on now to another
topic, having covered this last one more than I intended to. I
don't believe I need to explain myself further.

We will soon be on the road, Ellery Channing and
I that is, where we will meet Bradford in town and he
will join us on this last short trip before he turns the key
on one door to lock it forever and with a new key opens
another, also forever.

This has turned into quite a clandestine enterprise
and all three of us are up for it. You are the only one
who knows of our plans and I assure you we *will* be back
before the wedding. One of us is waiting for his new life
to begin.

Henry

Dear Henry,

I thank you more than I can say for spiriting
Bradford away. Your conspiracy with Mr. Channing was
brilliant. Mother and Father Althorp assumed he was
visiting a former classmate and he didn't disabuse them of
that notion.

Dearest Henry, this must be said, though I know
you will be uncomfortable with what I am about to
say. Thank you for always being the man who never
disappoints me no matter how much, how many times I
have disappointed you. I know that the news I brought to
you was hard and unexpected and I love you all the more
for your thoughtful answer to me and your unwavering
support, especially now as my wedding day draws near.

I will say no more but for this. I love you for who
you are, for who you *always* are, for who you will never
fail to be. My life will be less bright without you in it.

Mary

Dearest girl,

Thank you, thank you. You have ever been a joy to me, a great joy. I must close this letter now.

Dear Henry,

Bradford tells me you will be traveling with him and his mother and father to the church. I thought you were to meet all of us there, but perhaps it is wiser after all that you go with B. who will make sure that you don't get lost or suffer a sudden recurrence of the amnesia that seems to afflict you whenever you are asked to accompany a family member to church. It is a good thing that you are so well loved, else they would not put up with you and your nonsense.

I must go. There is much to do in these last few hours. I will see you soon for a short time only before the ceremony, and then Miss Mary Bright will be no more, and a Mrs. Bradford Althorp will take her place.

Henry, it is happening.

Mary

Dear Henry, dear friend,

I haven't quite found the words I want to say to you, but I know you well enough to know that you would prefer the fewer the better.

There was no one better, no one more fitting to stand next to me at the altar as Mary and I began our eternal life together as husband and wife. Short and to the point, Henry, as you would wish, but so much more left unexpressed.

I will miss you, Henry. You are everything I aspire to be.

With an abiding friendship and, yes, love,
Bradford Althorp

Dearest Henry, my dear Mr. Thoreau,

B. and I are departing for Europe this very hour.
When you receive this letter we will be well on our way.
My heart is too full to say more at this time, but for this.
If you had not been a part of my life for years I never
would have become Bradford's wife. Think upon what I
have just said and you will decipher my meaning. If not,
perhaps it is best as a mystery for you to ponder at a
different time, in a different place.

Right now I am about to board a ship, hence my
near illegible scrawl. My return to Concord for a visit
is yet to be determined but no one will hear of it sooner
than you. You are my last contact now, you will be the
first when I return.

I will close this letter and say no more but for this,
that I have loved you since I was a girl and will continue
to do so, ever and anon.

Mrs.Bradford Althorp, your Mary Bright

P.S. Give my love to our woodland friends and whistle
a tune for them in my name. If I could I would come
a-running to see them once again.

Dear Mary,

I am forwarding this letter to your London hotel. Hopefully it will reach you, but I think that it must, as Mr. Emerson and I have corresponded many times when he has been abroad, with no letters lost. We do not exchange billet-doux, at least I have received none from him nor have I sent any, and all is accounted for in our exchange of business and family letters.

My heart seems to have left me in the lurch and for the life of me I can't get it back. It is willful, this heart of mine, and often lulls me into a false sense of security, and I think that all is well when suddenly it quite abandons me when I am most in need of it.

I know you have not had this unsettling experience because of who you are. I am thinking now of the girl who styled herself "Miss Mary Bright", writing a letter to a man whom she had never met but had heard about, because curiosity got the better of her. I fear that, perchance, you have never got the better of me, much to my regret.

I wish that you could have known my beloved. She is strong as you are and as lovely. Be those things and more and always *Mary*, no one else, so that Bradford can have the full measure of you with all the wonder of who you are and all that you will be in all the years to come.

Well, I find that my heart is full after all, as are my eyes, so I cannot continue. When I saunter, I will miss you by my side. Tea cakes you have made, so pretty upon the plate, will lose a bit of their flavor and charm without you. But I will whistle to our woodland friends in your name when e'er I go there. And when you have some time to give, write me from London with your new address so that I may have the privilege of addressing the envelope "Mrs. Bradford Althorp". Goodby my Mary.

Henry David, your Mr. Thoreau

Well Thoreau, the little girl you knew is all grown up, leaving her parent's nest to be resettled in one of her own. And so it should be now that she is wed. Ricketson has invited us for a long stay at his shanty in the country and I have already accepted for you. We leave this afternoon, travel arrangements already made. You will not say no. Dinner provided by your mother and sister to eat along the way. Your goods, flute, a volume or two on the table by your bed I put into that threadbare dust rag that you call a satchel. I will call for you at 2:00 this afternoon at the house.

Yours ever, truly
Channing

Dear Channing,

If you are concerned for me with Mary gone now,
concerned that I will revisit those places in my mind
and heart where I have dwelt on loss too often, I say, all
is well dear friend. I am eternally resigned to my loss of
Ellen as if it were a heavenly decree which I have always
believed it must be. And Mary, the blessing of my life for
the last six years? She is another prize worthy of the gods,
but if anyone can best them Bradford Althorp can. As
Love's champion I lost the battle years ago and there is
no longer any fight left in me nor will there be. Who can
fight against the gods and win?

It will be a pleasure to see Ricketson again. I'll
be waiting by the gate, threadbare satchel in hand,
umbrella, &c.

Yours,
Thoreau

About the Author

Claire Russell received a Bachelor's Degree from the University of Wisconsin- Milwaukee with a double major in Art History and English Literature. She has spent most of her life trying to solve at least some of life's mysteries through studying, reading and writing, mostly poetry.

Other books by Claire Russell
One to Speak & One to Hear

More novels from Fomite...

Joshua Amses— *During This, Our Nadir*
Joshua Amses — *Ghatsr*
Joshua Amses — *Raven or Crow*
Joshua Amses — *The Moment Before an Injury*
Charles Bell — *The Married Land*
Charles Bell — *The Half Gods*
Jaysinh Birjepatel — *Nothing Beside Remains*
Jaysinh Birjepatel — *The Good Muslim of Jackson Heights*
David Brizer — *Victor Rand*
L. M Brown — *Hinterland*
Paula Closson Buck — *Summer on the Cold War Planet*
Dan Chodorkoff — *Loisaida*
Dan Chodorkoff — *Sugaring Down*
David Adams Cleveland — *Time's Betrayal*
Paul Cody— *Sphyxia*
Jaimee Wriston Colbert — *Vanishing Acts*
Roger Coleman — *Skywreck Afternoons*
Marc Estrin — *Hyde*
Marc Estrin — *Kafka's Roach*
Marc Estrin — *Speckled Vanities*
Marc Estrin — *The Annotated Nose*
Zdravka Evtimova — *In the Town of Joy and Peace*
Zdravka Evtimova — *Sinfonia Bulgarica*
Zdravka Evtimova — *You Can Smile on Wednesdays*
Daniel Forbes — *Derail This Train Wreck*
Peter Fortunato — *Carnevale*
Greg Guma — *Dons of Time*
Richard Hawley — *The Three Lives of Jonathan Force*
Lamar Herrin — *Father Figure*
Michael Horner — *Damage Control*
Ron Jacobs — *All the Sinners Saints*
Ron Jacobs — *Short Order Frame Up*
Ron Jacobs — *The Co-conspirator's Tale*
Scott Archer Jones — *And Throw Away the Skins*
Scott Archer Jones — *A Rising Tide of People Swept Away*
Julie Justicz — *Degrees of Difficulty*
Maggie Kast — *A Free Unsullied Land*
Darrell Kastin — *Shadowboxing with Bukowski*
Coleen Kearon — *#triggerwarning*

Coleen Kearon — *Feminist on Fire*
Jan English Leary — *Thicker Than Blood*
Diane Lefer — *Confessions of a Carnivore*
Diane Lefer — *Out of Place*
Rob Lenihan — *Born Speaking Lies*
Colin McGinnis — *Roadman*
Douglas W. Milliken — *Our Shadows' Voice*
Ilan Mochari — *Zinsky the Obscure*
Peter Nash — *Parsimony*
Peter Nash — *The Perfection of Things*
George Ovitt — *Stillpoint*
George Ovitt — *Tribunal*
Gregory Papadoyiannis — *The Baby Jazz*
Pelham — *The Walking Poor*
Andy Potok — *My Father's Keeper*
Frederick Ramey — *Comes A Time*
Joseph Rathgeber — *Mixedbloods*
Kathryn Roberts — *Companion Plants*
Robert Rosenberg — *Isles of the Blind*
Fred Russell — *Rafi's World*
Ron Savage — *Voyeur in Tangier*
David Schein — *The Adoption*
Lynn Sloan — *Principles of Navigation*
L.E. Smith — *The Consequence of Gesture*
L.E. Smith — *Travers' Inferno*
L.E. Smith — *Untimely RIPped*
Bob Sommer — *A Great Fullness*
Tom Walker — *A Day in the Life*
Susan V. Weiss —*My God, What Have We Done?*
Peter M. Wheelwright — *As It Is On Earth*
Suzie Wizowaty — *The Return of Jason Green*

Writing a review on Amazon, Good Reads, Shelfari, Library Thing or other social media sites for readers will help the progress of independent publishing. To submit a review, go to the book page on any of the sites and follow the links for reviews. Books from independent presses rely on reader-to-reader communications.

For more information or to order any of our books, visit:
http://www.fomitepress.com/our-books.html